The GARGOYLE

Garry Kilworth

Illustrated by Dan Williams

First published in Great Britain in 1997 by Mammoth
an imprint of Egmont Children's Books Limited
239 Kensington High Street, London W8 6SA

ISBN 0 7497 2889 2

10 9 8 7 6

A CIP catalogue record for this book is
available from the British Library

Printed in Great Britain by Cox & Wyman Ltd,
Reading, Berkshire

Contents

This book is for my grandson,
Alexander John
G.K.

For Leo, Tessa and Alice
D.W.

1 Stone comes to life

'TWAS MIDNIGHT and the great town clock scattered its chimes over the rooftops.

On the last stroke of twelve something dark and ugly stirred amongst a tower's Gothic spires. It was an awakening; an event which happened every full moon. Stone came to life, but high up, out of human sight. A strange shape shuddered, turned, clawed itself over a parapet, and sat for a moment in the secret darkness of the tower.

It was a gargoyle.

The creature sat and peered out into the night. On the other corners of the blackened, grimy monument were her three sisters. The gargoyle stared at one of them, stark in the moonlight.

It had a face of a wild beast, yet not like any living beast. Its lips were thick and brutish, framing jaws full of once-sharp teeth. High-pointed ears stuck out like those of a lynx from the sides of its head. It had short bat-wings on its powerful shoulders. Its forelimbs stuck out in front of it, as thick and strong as those of any panther. There were no paws, however, but the open talons of a giant eagle.

The gargoyle's study of her stone sister was interrupted by the sound of footsteps. A human was hurrying past the monument on the street below. Soon the sound died away and all was still again.

The gargoyle was wary of humans. Yet, at the same time, she was curious. It seemed to her that there could be no real harm in such puny creatures. She had several times encountered one, without being recognised herself. On all occasions she had been mistaken for a large black dog and had slunk into the shadows.

Before the dawn crept with soft grey paws over the rooftops of the city, the gargoyle had to be back on her perch, her hindquarters buried deep in the tower's stone. If she failed to return on time, she knew instinctively that her body would shatter like glass under the hammer of daybreak. With this in mind she set forth on this autumn midnight, down the inner steps of the tower to the streets below.

It had been raining shortly before she descended from the tower and the streets were dark and shiny. The smell of wet leaves came up from the gutters. The air was heavy, damp, still. The gargoyle slipped into an alley and made her way towards the park. In the middle of the alley the gargoyle encountered a house cat.

On seeing the gargoyle, the cat's eyes widened.

The tabby's legs went as stiff and straight

as stilts. Its fur stood up on end and it hissed and spat at the gargoyle. It turned in a tense and awkward manner, keeping the gargoyle in view the whole time. The gargoyle wanted nothing to do with stupid cats. She went on by, her great stone claws falling soft on the mossy cobbles.

Once she had passed, the cat sped away into the night.

'What are you doing out at this time?' said a voice suddenly, as the gargoyle reached the end of the alley.

She peered out of the exit to see a policeman speaking to a man who was none too steady on his feet.

'What's it to you?' said the man aggressively. 'Free country, isn't it?'

The gargoyle understood these words and could have answered herself, if she had been asked the question. How she came to know language was not clear to her, though

she must have heard ten thousand voices in the time she had been on the monument. Daily, visitors to the tower leaned over the high balcony and talked to one another, not a metre above the gargoyle's ears.

Perhaps she had soaked up language like a sponge, over the many years she had been on the monument.

'Now, now, no need to take that tone of voice with me. You've had one too many, sir. Off you go home now. You don't want to be a bother to anyone, do you?' said the policeman.

The policeman sent the man on his way with these words.

The man staggered off in the direction of a housing estate and the policeman sighed and continued his beat.

The gargoyle knew what the policeman was thinking: that it was lonely out in the streets while all others were in their houses, most of them asleep. It was a quiet world, perhaps a dangerous world sometimes, with muggers and burglars abroad. The policeman was bored, yet he had to be alert.

She felt lonely too, though she was not frightened of any criminals who might be in the alleys and streets. There was something inside the gargoyle which cried out for company. All her life she had been alone, with no one to share her thoughts, no one to pass the time of night.

The gargoyle longed for a living companion of some kind. Her sisters were all stone. They remained stone, even under the hunter's moon. She had tried speaking to them, but they remained deaf, blind and dumb on their separate corners of the tower.

When the downpour came, water flowed into the lead gutters, through the hollow forms of the gargoyles, and gushed from their cavernous mouths. Rainwater, but no words, came out. They gargled nonsense at her. When the sun came out again their mouths remained locked open, the wind whistling through their worn, broken teeth. They were poor companions.

So on this night the gargoyle suddenly decided she was going to speak to a human.

And who better to speak to than the policeman? For he was an official of the law and must have seen many strange things in his working life. He roamed the night streets, just like the gargoyle. He was expected to keep his head in all emergencies, remaining calm and in control. The policeman was the perfect person for the gargoyle to approach on its first real meeting with a human being.

She stepped out of the alley and said,

‘Good evening, constable. A fine night now the rain has ceased to fall, is it not?’

The policeman, who had been whistling, stopped dead in his tracks. His whistle froze on his lips. His eyes started out of his head. Disappointingly for the gargoyle he turned to stone himself, for a short while. Then he came to life again a few moments later and backed away, staring.

'Crikey,' whispered the policeman. 'A black panther – or – or something.'

'A talking panther – or – something?' suggested the gargoyle.

But the policeman started making a terrible racket, yelling and screaming for help into his radio. He had got out his truncheon and was waving it in front of him, as if he expected the gargoyle to attack him. After a few minutes two patrol cars came screeching up the street and more policemen jumped out. The gargoyle thought it was time to run.

They chased her the length of the street in their cars. The gargoyle began leaping fences into people's gardens in an effort to escape. The policemen clambered over barriers after her. She had no idea what they would do if they caught up with her, but she did not want to find out.

A few of the policemen had weapons and she was afraid someone was going to get hurt.

Finally, in desperation, she climbed a sheer wall, using her wings to assist her. She could not fly, as such, but flapping her wings helped make her body lighter.

She clawed her way up the brickwork on to a rooftop. Once there she ran skittering and skidding across the slates, making a terrible clatter. One or two loose slates went skimming silently out into the night air. They smashed on the concrete below. Her stony claws scratched at the wet, slippery roof, which threatened every second to send her crashing in the wake of the slates.

With the aid of her large talons, and flapping her bat-wings for balance, she managed to climb higher and grip the ridge which ran the length of the roof.

A surprised moon watched her progress.

She walked along until she came to an open dormer window. She slipped inside this window, between the fluttering curtains and fell heavily on to a carpeted floor in a strange room. The place was in deep darkness, yet someone else was there.

2 A companion

ALL SEEMED QUIET in the room. Outside was pandemonium.

The gargoyle could hear the police charging through the streets. There were distant shouts. Cars sped by, their lights clawing at the darkness in front of them. Gradually, all sounds faded away on the night.

The room remained still for a time, then the sound of sobbing came to the gargoyle and she could smell the musty odours of tears on human skin, of damp breath.

'Are you crying because of me?' asked the gargoyle, in her deep throaty tones. 'If you are, I shall leave.'

There was stillness for a moment, then a

choked voice said, 'No – not because of you. I'm too upset to care about an old dog getting in my room. I wasn't crying though. You didn't hear me crying. I was just making a noise in my sleep. Boys my age don't cry. There was another long silence, then the words. 'How – how come you can talk?'

'How is it that *you* can talk?' countered the gargoyle.

'I learned when I was a baby,' said the voice in an aggrieved tone.

'Well, I learned from people,' said the gargoyle. 'People taught me to understand speech.' She paused before adding, 'I was never a baby. The mason carved me out of granite carried from a quarry far away. I think the block of stone must have been used for magic, because I come to life every full moon. Perhaps an ancient wizard used it as a table for his spells. Or spilled some

enchanted potion on a rock. Who knows? Here I am and talking as well as any boy who learned as a baby.'

'I don't care about magic,' said the boy from the darkness of his bed. 'I just want my mum back home.'

'Good for you,' said the gargoyle. 'If I had a mother, I should want her back too.'

The boy sniffed then asked the gargoyle a question.

'If you're not a dog, what are you?'

'I'm a rather ugly gargoyle.'

The boy said, 'An ugly gargoyle? All gargoyles are ugly. I've seen them on churches. They're gross.'

'Is that short for grotesque? I believe I'm

grotesque. I rather like being grotesque. It has dignity, that word. I could be absurd but I'm not. I'm grotesque. What are you?'

'I'm good-looking,' said the boy, emphatically. 'Nothing wrong with me.'

'There's nothing wrong with me, either,' said the gargoyle, huffily, 'apart from a little erosion.'

The boy seemed to hesitate before asking, 'What's erosion?'

'Wear and tear on the stonework, you know,' sighed the gargoyle, enjoying her first real conversation. 'Wind and rain, out in all weathers, can't fail to cause a blurring of the outline, can it? Acid rain, too. That's a killer. Kills the trees, the grass, and causes my back to become pitted. It's almost destroyed my wings completely, and my claws . . . '

'Claws?' said the boy. 'You have claws? And wings?'

'Bat-wings.'

'Bat-wings,' breathed the boy. 'That's cool.'

'It's got nothing to do with my temperature,' sniffed the gargoyle. 'I'm stone. I'm attacked by the cold and the heat, and rain beating on my head, wearing me away, slowly, gradually, until one day, I suppose, I shall be no more than a pebble to be cast away on a beach somewhere.'

'Look,' said the boy, 'my name's Alexander. They call me Alex for short. What's your name?'

The gargoyle considered this very reasonable question and found she could not answer it.

'I don't have a name. I'm just a piece of masonry – a chunk of carved granite with a lead pipe for a gullet. Creatures like me are called things like "gargoyle", but we don't

have personal names.'

'I want to see you,' said Alex, moving in his bed. 'I'm going to switch on the light.'

The gargoyle considered this and remembered the actions of the policeman. It was better not to be seen, she thought, at least until the boy got used to her. Better to remain a part of the darkness in the room, unseen, disembodied. No matter how much she might prepare her new companion for the sight of her features, it would be a great shock. She had to dissuade him from wanting to see her for the moment.

'The light – the light does things to me,' she said. 'I don't like the light.'

'Migraine,' Alex said. 'I expect you get migraines. Bright lights give my mum migraines. She gets bad headaches from it.'

'I was thinking more along the lines that I might dissolve in light,' the gargoyle muttered. 'Melt completely away.'

'That – or get a headache,' Alex said, sounding equally satisfied with both reasons.

She got the impression that the boy was not all that keen either on turning on the light. Perhaps he thought it was too soon for such a measure. Maybe he believed he was having a strange dream and that he would wake if he turned on the light. That was the most likely explanation. In any case, he made no further move towards the switch and seemed happy to remain lying back in his bed, talking to her.

The gargoyle settled down on the rug and peered around the room. Now that her eyes had got used to the dark she could see the boy liked books. There were three shelves of books on one wall. There were also games of different kinds. A pile of comics spilled over the edge of a cardboard box.

'Why were you – er – upset about your mother?' asked the gargoyle, eventually.

Alex sighed. 'My mum was in an accident at work. She got badly burned with cleaning chemicals. Now she's in hospital and I haven't seen her since they took her away.'

'I'm sorry to hear that,' said the gargoyle.

'But she'll get better, won't she?'

'Well, my dad says it'll take a long time. She's already been there seven weeks and it might take a few months. He's only been to see her twice. Dad's out of work, see, and Mum's in a special hospital that treats people for burns. It's well over a hundred kilometres away. We can't afford the fares to go there, not both of us. We haven't got a car, see. Dad says I can go in a few weeks – maybe.'

The gargoyle nodded her great head, slowly, in sympathy.

'Now I can see why you're unhappy. You would like to visit your mother to tell her to get well soon.'

Alex said, 'I want her to get better, but it's not just that. We had a row, see, before she had the accident. I wanted a pair of trainers and she said we couldn't afford it, so I shouted and sulked. I didn't get to say

I was sorry. I feel rotten about it. She – she thinks I don't like her.'

'Hmmm,' said the gargoyle. 'You could ask your father to carry a message for you, couldn't you?'

'I have done,' Alex replied, 'but she couldn't talk when he went last – her face got all burned up – and anyway, he said he didn't want to bother her with my problems until she was a bit better. I know she's just lying there thinking.'

The gargoyle folded her taloned forelegs over one another and bowed her mighty head in thought. She had never strayed outside the city. Mostly, she went to the park where there were living things to enjoy.

She liked to be amongst the trees and shrubs, close to the ducks and geese on the pond, watching the foxes glide like phantoms through the night, studying the movements of hedgehogs, snakes, mice and all manner of mammals, birds and reptiles.

Yet there was nothing to stop her from travelling across the countryside, if she so wished, so long as she was back before the dawn.

'Do you know the way to this hospital?' she asked the boy.

Alex sat up in bed. 'I could find it – on the map. I learned to read maps in the scouts and I know the name of the town. Why?'

'Perhaps we could go there,' she murmured. 'It would be a wonderful adventure, wouldn't it?'

He went silent for quite a while, then he said, 'How?'

'You could ride on my back. I'm very fast on my feet, when I have to be. We have about six hours until dawn. I think we could do it, if we went now.'

The moon had moved over the sky and was now shining through the gap between the curtains into the bedroom. The gargoyle knew she was spotlighted by its bright beams. Alex could see her shape now, as she lay on the rug.

'You're – you're very big,' Alex faltered.

'Yes,' she said.

'You – you don't eat things, do you? I mean, you're not a carnivore?'

'I don't have to eat,' replied the gargoyle. 'I'm made of stone. At the moment, it's living stone, but tomorrow when the sun comes up, I shall turn back into a solid statue again.'

'So you don't have to kill things?'

'I have never harmed a creature in my whole existence.'

Alex suddenly reached out and turned on his bedside light. The gargoyle was revealed in all its ugliness now. She watched the boy's face for signs of panic.

He was a wiry-looking boy, smaller than average, with a great shock of ginger hair. His face had more freckles than the Milky Way had stars.

'Do I frighten you?' she asked.

'A bit,' whispered Alex.

'I look horrible,' she nodded.

'Not horrible exactly – what you said before – grotesque,' Alex explained.

'A dignified grotesque?' she asked.

Alex said, 'I suppose so.'

'But not absurd? Not ridiculous?'

'No, not that,' confirmed Alex.

The gargoyle was happy with this reply.

'Could you ride on my back, do you think? Or would that terrify you too much?'

Alex's mouth set in a firm line, then he said, 'If I want to see my mum, I'll have to, won't I?'

Alex got out of bed. 'I'll have to sneak downstairs, to get the map. You wait here. I don't want my dad seeing you. He'd have a fit. Dad's asleep in the bedroom along the landing. I don't think he'll wake up. He's a heavy sleeper.'

Alex crept out of the room and disappeared into the darkness beyond. A few minutes later he was back again, with the book of maps in his hand. He put this down for a moment while he pulled on his underclothes, jeans and sweater. Then he put some socks and worn trainers on. Finally he was ready.

He now looked doubtfully at the gargoyle, still spread like a black panther over the rug. He soon conquered his fears though, because he climbed on her back and tucked his skinny legs under her bat-wings.

The gargoyle experienced the unusual sensation of feeling the boy astride her

It was true it aroused panic in her breast, which fluttered there like a trapped wild bird. But she also discovered a kind of warm, comfortable feeling, as if contact with the boy was right, as if they were meant to ride the night together, boy and mythical beast.

'There's not much to grip,' said Alex, feeling around her stone neck.

'Get hold of my ears,' she replied. 'They're quite stiff and it won't hurt me. I'll lower my wings to hold you on tight, because we'll be going quite fast.'

'Very fast,' said Alex, excitedly, 'if we want to be back here before dawn.'

'Precisely,' the gargoyle replied.

A few moments later they were out in the moonlight. They were high up, on a tenement rooftop, with smaller houses and buildings all around and below them.

The gargoyle began walking along the

ridge of the roof, but this particular place was slippery with moss. Suddenly the gargoyle lost its footing. It went skidding down the slick roof like a skier down a snowy slope. The terrified Alex clung to her ears and yelled, 'We're going to fall!'

The gargoyle hoped she would be able to clutch the gutter, but missed – and went sailing out into the darkness.

3 The night flight

'HOLD ON!' CRIED the gargoyle. She struggled with her wings. They were stretched to their fullest extent. With great luck the pair were over a cluster of chimneys. There were fires down below and a draught of warm air came up. It lifted the gargoyle long enough for her to be able to glide down to a flat roof below.

They hit the roof at a run and the gargoyle managed to make a landing. She stopped to get her breath and her confidence back. Her legs went very shaky when she realised how close they had been to falling all the way down to the street.

'Don't do that again,' whispered Alex in fright, thinking the gargoyle had done it on purpose.

They continued their journey over the top of the town. Alex was stiff with fright at first and he kept looking down the slopes of the roofs to the street below, but after a while he relaxed. The excitement took over from the fear and he began to point out landmarks.

'There's the town hall over there. If we follow the road that runs past it, we'll soon be outside the city.'

'Good,' said the gargoyle, 'but we must leave the roads as soon as possible and travel over the countryside.'

They moved over a strange, ancient landscape of chimney pots, flat roofs, peaked houses and spires. The gargoyle leaped from gable to eaves, from roof to roof, gliding silently over the chasms. Sometimes she used her wings to help her, in which case Alex had to grip her ears

tightly. They seemed to float through the night together, from stack to stack, turret to turret, house to house. The gargoyle was amazed at her own agility, but then she had long known her talons and wings were good tools.

She crossed the city in this way, like a heavy-footed ghost, over the tiles and along the gutters of a sleeping population. Black shadows jumped into hidden nooks and crannies, moonlight sprang shining on to blue slate, revealing the path ahead of them. They weaved through forests of television aerials. They slipped past washing poles and dovecotes.

Finally it was time to descend to the ground.

Alex consulted his map in the moonlight, as they clattered down an outside fire escape to the street below.

'We can follow the motorway southwards,' he told the gargoyle. 'Once we reach it. We don't need to go on the road itself – we can run alongside it, out in the fields – away from the lights.'

'Excellent,' said the gargoyle.

They ran at a brisk pace along the pavements out of the town, passing buildings and housing estates. Alex had on darkish clothes, and the dirt and grime on the gargoyle meant that if they kept to the shadows they could not easily be seen.

Cars flashed past them, headlights probing the road ahead. The night rider on his weird mount slipped by one or two pedestrians who were aware of a shape sliding through the darkness, but were unable to identify it. Soon they were out in the fields and heading for a distant motorway.

Time was the enemy. Time had to be defeated.

The gargoyle had to be back on her perch before the dawn rays struck her form, or she would shatter into a thousand shards of useless gravel. She was aware of this in some way, though she could not have said how she came by the knowledge.

The gargoyle had many feelings, many memories she did not understand. They came to her through the music from churches, when the vibrant organs swelled with sound. They came to her on night breezes, out of old stone, out of worn wood. They trickled into her from oak beams, from beech pews, from brass bells and iron rings. They seeped into her from marble arches, from granite buttresses and high limestone spires. They crept into her as holy colours from stained-glass windows.

In this way did the gargoyle come by her small understanding of who she was and what would be her fate.

'Quickly, quickly,' cried Alex, the wind in his red hair, the lights of the distant motorway streaming by them.

Over bog and field, through spinney and wood, the couple sped. Sometimes the moon appeared cracked and crazed through the branches of trees. At other times it was bright and full, laying out their way before them. Across moor, over bridges, under tunnels ran the gargoyle. Over hills, along valleys. Her great claws gripped the earth driving her forward.

A tramp who saw them thunder by gave out a startled yell and went down on his knees in fright.

Anyone seeing the dreadful vision of the gargoyle in full gallop, and a wild boy clinging to her back, shouting fiercely and waving encouragement with flailing arms, might have been forgiven for sending up a sudden prayer to the heavens.

They were indeed a terrible sight, the pair of them, as they travelled the night on their mission.

'Hurry, hurry,' cried Alex.

At times she was in danger of sinking in marsh, but she thrashed her wings to lighten her massive form. She used her bat-wings again when they met a fence, hedge or wall, sailing over them with the ease of a hunting horse.

Alex clung to her ears at such times, his body bouncing on her back.

4 Journey's end

FINALLY, AFTER TWO hours of hard riding, the pair came to the edge of a brightly lit town. Alex looked at his map and found where the hospital stood. Once again they took to the rooftops, until they reached their destination.

Then Alex dismounted.

The pair of them crept past the windows of the hospital, looking for the ward where Alex's mother lay. Alex knew the name of it from his father. Eventually they found it. The gargoyle prised open a window with her strong claws.

The gargoyle watched from outside as Alex crept through the ward. The boy came to a bed and paused there, looking at a photograph of a man and boy on the locker. The gargoyle could see that the picture was of Alex and had no doubt the man was his father.

A woman lay sleeping in the bed. Her face was terribly raw and scarred on one side, while the other side was pretty. Alex shook her gently and whispered into her ear.

'Mum, Mum – it's me, Alex.'

The woman woke, gradually, murmuring, 'Wh-what is it? Is it time for my medicine?'

'No, Mum, it's me, Alex. I've come for a visit.

His mother opened her eyes and stared at her son's face in the moonlight streaming through the windows. She looked surprised and worried, especially when she glanced at the clock. It said half-past three in the morning.

'Alex? What are you doing here at this time?'

'I – I got a lift from a friend. They're waiting outside to take me back. I just wanted to see you, Mum.'

'Waiting? In a car? Does your dad know you're here?'

Alex shook his head. 'No, he doesn't, Mum – please don't tell him. I'm all right, honest. I just wanted to see you. I wanted to say sorry for that row we had. I don't want the rotten old trainers now – I just want you home.'

Tears shone in his mother's eyes as she reached out and gently touched his cheek.

'Oh, you poor boy – fancy having a mother like me – a mother who leaves you.'

'You couldn't help it,' Alex said, his own voice close to tears. 'It was an accident. Me and Dad, we're fine, don't you worry about that. But we want you home all the same. I know it's not going to be for a while yet, but I just wanted you to say you didn't hate me for that row.'

'You silly boy,' she said. Then she smiled, 'Of course I don't hate you.'

The gargoyle, staring through the window, could tell that having to smile hurt her face, but she had done it anyway.

She said, 'You'd better be careful – the

nurse will be coming on her rounds soon. Are you sure you've got someone to take you back? You haven't run away or anything?'

'No, nothing like that, Mum,' said Alex, shaking his head fiercely. 'I told you – a friend's taking me.'

'It must be a very good friend to come out at this time of night.'

'Yes – very good,' said Alex, glancing towards the window.

The gargoyle swelled with pride when she heard this. She was a friend to someone. She belonged to a real family. A human boy had accepted her into his heart.

Alex's mother looked towards the window.

'There's someone out there,' she said. 'I can see a shape at the window.'

'It's just my friend,' said Alex quickly. Then, to distract his mother, he asked,

'Mum, are you getting better? Will you be coming home soon?'

She turned back towards her son. 'Oh, I hope so, Alex. I do hope so. Is your father managing?'

'Oh, yeah – we get on great together, don't you worry about us. We're fine. We just want you back because – because we're a family, see. Dad's looking forward to you coming home. He says we can take a bit of a holiday, somewhere cheap, when you get out. Maybe we could go camping or something? That doesn't cost much, does it?'

Alex's mother changed her position then, turning her face to the wall.

'You'd better go now,' she said, 'before the nurse comes.'

Alex started to move towards the door, but then he turned again.

'Mum, what's the matter?' he asked.

She was silent for a few moments, but then she said, 'My face – I'm going to be like this for some time – perhaps for always.'

'Me and Dad don't mind that, Mum – you know.'

'But other people will stare at me. I – I look grotesque.'

Alex glanced towards the window again and the gargoyle knew what her young friend was feeling and thinking. He was recalling their earlier conversation, she was sure. Alex might be small of stature, but he had a big heart and he was bright enough to pick up on things that mattered.

Alex said to his mother, 'Grotesque? There's a lot of dignity in that, Mum. Thing is, you don't look absurd, if you know what I mean. You don't look ridiculous. Famous artists made grotesque statues, didn't they? Artists don't make things unless they think they're worthwhile, do they?'

His mother turned her face towards him again, an expression of surprise on her features.

'What?' she asked, faintly.

'Well, I mean – dignity and all that! It's how you hold yourself, isn't it? How you feel as well.'

She murmured, 'Oh, Alex, come here.'

He went back to her and they hugged one another, hard.

Then, with shining eyes, she told him to go quickly. Alex ran across the ward because he could hear the soft tread of the night nurse, as she walked across her office floor at the end of the ward. The gargoyle was gratified to see Alex slip into the shadows just beyond the double doors when the nurse left the office to begin her ward round.

Once Alex was back on the gargoyle again, they began their return journey to the city.

5 Galloping for the dawn

IT WAS A race against the night. They had to beat the darkness to the dawn. The consequences of being late were too horrible to consider.

The gargoyle retraced her journey at great speed, though she had to be careful that the tired Alex did not fall off. In the middle of a field the gargoyle stopped to question the way. It was then their unfortunate position revealed itself. Alex, frantically poring over his map, had to admit that they must have taken a wrong turning at some point.

They were lost.

'I think it was back at that wood, when we left the motorway and started over the fields. I'm – I'm a bit sleepy. It's my fault.'

He was, in fact, exhausted through lack of rest.

'We can't go back,' said the gargoyle, anxiously. 'There's no time to go back.'

Alex studied the map once again.

'I'll have to guess where we are then, by some landmarks. Can you see a water tower anywhere? A big one. It's here on the map, so we should be able to see it.'

'No,' said the despairing gargoyle, desperately searching the horizon for signs of a tower. 'All I can see are hills around us.'

Alex looked up, squinting. 'No buildings? There must be some buildings.'

'No,' replied the gargoyle. 'Only countryside. Doesn't the map show hills then?'

'Yes it does,' admitted Alex, 'but I'm not that good at reading contour lines. I mean, you have to know the heights and all that. Maybe we should go in that direction,' he pointed. 'That feels right.'

'But what if it's wrong?' groaned the gargoyle, flapping her wings in worry. 'What if it's not the right way?'

Alex looked at her bleakly. 'I don't know – I'm sorry. You shouldn't have brought me, should you? There wasn't enough time, really. I shouldn't have let you bring me – I should've said no. I could've persuaded you not to.'

The gargoyle knew this was not true. Once she had made up her mind to take Alex to his mother, nothing could have prevented her, not even her own qualms. A determined gargoyle is unstoppable. It seals its own fate with its obstinacy. She was certain that all gargoyles must be as stubborn as she was, simply because of their natural state. Being hewn from solid rock, a thing of stone, she was by her very nature a rigid creature.

'No, it's not your fault, it's mine,' she sighed. 'But you may have to go the rest of the way on your own. I – I might soon shatter into pieces.'

Just at that moment there was a noise overhead. The gargoyle was too depressed to take much notice of it, but Alex looked up and he suddenly let out a whoop of joy.

'A plane!' he shouted.

'So what if it is?' sighed the gargoyle.

'Don't you see?' cried Alex. 'It's heading towards the city airport. That's the way we go – the same way as the plane. Come on, we've still got time . . . '

Heartened by these words from her rider, the gargoyle set off in pursuit of the aeroplane. She had seen it go in a straight line across the sky and she took the same direction. A village was in their path but they went straight through. The postman on his way to work fell off his bicycle when he saw a live gargoyle with a boy on its back.

They crossed farmlands at the back of the village, over dykes and ditches, through bracken and gorse. Finally the city limits came into view, but they could see light creeping between the walls of the tower blocks at the back of town. It seemed that time was against them. They were going to fail.

'Too late!' cried the gargoyle. 'I'm not going to make it back to the monument!'

'Don't give up hope!' cried the boy on her back. 'Something might save you yet.'

The gargoyle, breathlessly racing towards the streets of the city, moaned, 'What could possibly save me now?'

Just at that moment black clouds began to roll swiftly across the sky. A storm was coming in, bringing its own darkness. Soon the heavens were thick with cumulus and the dawn was held at bay. It might have been a miracle except that it happened quite often in autumn. So far as Alex and the gargoyle were concerned, it was a marvel, but then that was because they needed it. The rumble of thunder followed. Then the rain came down like nails.

The gargoyle reached the filthy monument, still dark with age and soot from now-dead chimneys.

'Don't worry about me,' said Alex, jumping off. 'I'll find my own way home.'

The gargoyle started to race up the stone steps, but then she heard Alex call to her.

'How can I pay you back for what you've done?'

She turned on the top step and replied, 'I've never been part of a family. I want to be part of yours. I'll come to you next full moon and you can tell me stories about how families live. Ordinary stories about everyday life. I would like that above all.'

‘I promise you will hear them,’ called Alex. ‘I promise.’

The gargoyle ran to the edge of the tower. A shaft of sunlight was just piercing the clouds in the east. It struck earth like a golden pillar thrown from heaven. Her limbs began to stiffen, her body crackled. She crawled over the parapet, fighting the firm feeling.

She sank to her hindquarters into the stone tower, just as it was turning solid. One or two cracks appeared on her neck. Several more down her flank. They were little fissures, zigzagging like forked lightning down her length. Some stone dust fell, a chip or two dropped, but nothing more.

Then, finally, she was safely in place, though an expert eye might have noticed that her position was just slightly out of true compared with the other three gargoyles on the tower. This hardly mattered, because she knew that people never stared at gargoyles. They glanced, they winced at the ugliness, and then they turned their attention to prettier architecture.

The gargoyle could not wait until the next full moon, when she was to receive her reward in the stories of ordinary life.

6 The new gargoyles

IT HAPPENED THAT before the next full moon, the monument was cleaned for the first time in two hundred years. The city council had been cleaning many of the buildings in the past and it was now the turn of the statues and monuments.

A stone-cleaning firm came.

They used strong cleaning chemicals and detergents. Grime was scoured away, dirt was eaten away. Soon the stone sparkled, having been reinstated in its original pale colour.

As the end of the month drew near, a cleanliness crept over the monument. It appeared that the gargoyles would be the last to be scrubbed. On the night of the full moon, the gargoyle still had not been cleaned, but she was afraid to leave the tower in case they missed her. What if she came back in the morning and found all the rest of the stone spotless, while she still had the grime and dirt of ages on her stone? They would guess there was something strange about her then. She would stand out amongst the others like an unwashed urchin among shining choir-boys.

So she was unable to leave the tower and was indeed restored to her original sanitary state that night.

She had her claws sharpened, her wings trimmed, her teeth replaced. Before the stone-cutters left she had been returned to the fierce-looking mythical beast she had been when the tower was first erected. Now she looked more than grotesque, she looked savage and ruthless as well.

When the full moon finally came round again she left the tower in high excitement, but she was no sooner in the streets below than a loud hue and cry broke out. It seemed the stone-cleaners and cutters had not done her any favours. Her bleached form could easily be seen, even when she slipped into the shadows.

There was nowhere for her to hide now, as she travelled the night. Dogs growled and barked at her, people screamed and called for help, cats collected in gangs and harassed her. She could not get more than a hundred metres from the monument without being chased back again.

Not only was she pale and wan, easily seen even in the darkest of alleys, she looked very ferocious. There was no mistaking that she had a huge mouthful of sharp fangs. It was noticed that her great talons were like stone spikes. Her powerful ridged muscles revealed her strength. The bat-wings drew attention to her mythical status.

So, in the end, she had to go back to her place on the tower, even during the full moon. She could roam the streets of the city no longer. Because she had been seen now, several times, and no one quite knew what she was, the police were out looking for her, scouring the alleys with their trained dogs, armed with all sorts of weapons.

She could not go to her friend, Alex, and hear the stories he had promised her.

Another full moon came and went.

The temperature dropped as the weather adopted harsher manners. Snow settled on the gargoyle's head. Ice hardened between her teeth. Her eyes glazed over with frozen mists and her wings grew heavy with the weight of winter. Cold penetrated her stone heart and her new cracks were attacked by the frost that came in the early dark of mornings.

They closed and locked the gates to the monument's viewing tower for the winter months.

The gargoyle was saddened by her new circumstances. She felt she was as much a prisoner as her sisters. They were all fixed to the tower. Stone in stone. It was worse for her, because the others were not aware of the world. She had walked among mortals, and even befriended one. She had known the freedom of movement. Now all that was denied her.

One day, when the world was dim and hazy, with a thick mist hiding the houses and streets, the gargoyle was staring dispiritedly into the gloom. Her spirit was heavy. A great melancholy had filled her, which threatened to make her so miserable she believed she would never feel joy again.

She peered into the murk without a grain of hope in her hollow breast.

Then, out of the corner of her eye she saw something scaling the side of the tower. Because she could not turn her head, she was unable to see who or what it was, but she realised a dark shape was climbing up the stonework. Bit by bit, the figure got higher and higher, until the gargoyle feared for the creature's life. Then, finally, the figure reached the gargoyles and pulled itself over the parapet on to the balcony.

After a few moments the gargoyle heard a familiar voice.

'I can see why you didn't come again. I expect you can't come down now that you're clean. I had to wait until a foggy day, so no one would see me climbing up. Don't worry, I'm a good climber – I practise on the abseil wall in the gym.'

She almost turned her head, despite the fact that it was not full moon, or even night. Her spirit lifted though, and she felt a quiver of happiness run through her form. The voice, of course, belonged to Alex. He had come to her, now that she could not go to him. He had remembered which corner of the tower belonged to her and he was there on the balcony.

'I don't suppose you can speak to me,' said Alex, 'but that doesn't matter, does it? I wasn't able to come sooner, because Mum came home and we've been pretty

busy since. She's a lot better now, and Dad's got some work – only a couple of days a week, but it's better than nothing. Mum's still got her scars but the hospital's going to help her with those.'

Alex paused for a moment and leaned his elbow on the parapet, as if settling down for a good while.

'Anyway,' he said, 'I've come to tell you

about those things I promised. About ordinary life and everything. Seems a bit boring to me, but then I'm not a gargoyle. I suppose it's opposites, isn't it? You have your magic, which is just ordinary to you, so my normal life is interesting. Well, here goes, you asked for it.'

And the wonderful stories about ordinary life began.

If you enjoyed this

MAMMOTH READ try:

Seth and the Strangers

Jenny Nimmo
Illustrated by *Peter Melnyczuk*

A dark cloud rains tiny whirling shapes on to the hills. Seth knows each spinning silver disc carries something extraordinary. Something no one on earth has ever before encountered . . .

Where have they come from?
What do they want?

A science fiction fantasy set in the wilds of the Yorkshire countryside.

If you enjoyed this
MAMMOTH READ try:

Ghost Blades

Anthony Masters
Illustrated by *Chris Price*

Terry is speeding down the street, twisting and turning on his friend's Rollerblades. They are so light he almost feels he has perfect control. Then the blades take over – propelling him through an overgrown garden and into a sinister-looking house.

A tense and exciting ghost story to send shivers down your spine.